BLACK BEAUTY

ANNA SEWELL

BOOKS

Editor: Heather Hammonds
Cover Illustration: Terry Riley
Illustrations: Terry Riley
Typesetting: Midland Typesetters

Black Beauty
First published in 2007 by
Budget Books Pty Ltd
45–55 Fairchild Street
Heatherton Victoria 3202 Australia

ISBN: 978 1 7418 1476 7

Printed & bound in India

The Author
Anna Sewell

Anna Sewell (1820–1878) was born in Norfolk, England.

Black Beauty was the only book that Anna wrote. The story was her way of campaigning against the cruel treatment of many working horses in the nineteenth century.

The book made an important early contribution to the international movement to prevent cruelty to animals.

Anna was disabled as a youngster and often walked with the aid of a crutch. But she was an expert rider and a great animal lover.

The model for Black Beauty was her brother's horse, Bessie.

Anna didn't live to see her book become a classic that would be enjoyed by future generations of children all around the world. She died, just three months after it was published.

Anna's story has been made into numerous films and television series.

Her mother, Mary Sewell, was also a children's author.

Contents

The horse world has a language of its own.
You will find these words in the story.

breaking in – training a horse for riding or pulling a carriage

colt – a young male horse

bearing rein – a leather strap used to force a horse to hold its head in a high, arched position

bit – the piece of metal in a horse's mouth that is linked to the reins and bridle – used to guide a horse

bridle – a leather harness that attaches to a horse's head

blacksmith – a person who makes iron shoes for horses

grazing – feeding on grass

groom – a person who looks after horses

harness – a collar and straps attached to a horse so it can pull a carriage or wagon

mane – the hair growing on top of a horse's head and neck

mare – a female horse

reins – long leather straps attached to the bit and bridle

walk, trot, canter and gallop – a walk is a horse's slowest pace; a trot is a jogging movement, just faster than a walk; a canter is a gentle gallop; a gallop is a horse's racing speed.

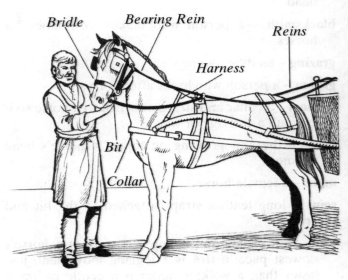

Introduction

My name is Black Beauty and this is the story of my life.

When this book was written, more than one hundred years ago, the life of working horses was often hard and cruel. We worked long hours and many of us became ill, or died from exhaustion.

Some owners did not know how to look after us properly. Others simply did not care about us. They replaced us when we were no longer of any use to them.

I have had many owners. Most were kind, good people. They made sure I was treated very well. I grew to love them – and the grooms and stable boys who worked for them.

But a few of my owners treated me very badly. They made my life one of pain and misery.

I have known many good horses in my lifetime too. There was my mother, Duchess, and my brother, Rob Roy. Then, of course, there was Merrylegs and Ginger.

We spent a lot of happy times together, when we were young. I shall never forget any of them. And I don't think you will either, after you have read my story . . .

My name is Black Beauty.

Chapter 1
My First Home

Farmer Gray was my first master. I was born on his farm.

My first memories are of lying in a lush green meadow. In the corner of the meadow was a pond of cool clear water, with shady trees hanging over it.

On hot days my mother and I would stand in the pond to cool down. And when it was cold, we had a small wooden shed where we could shelter from the frost and wind.

When I got a little older, my mother went to work each day. But she always came back to me in the evening.

There were six other colts in the meadow with us. They were all older than me. Some were almost grown up horses.

I loved to run around the meadow with the colts. Around and around we went, as fast as we could gallop. There was rough play too. Sometimes we would nip and bite each other.

We stood in the pond.

My mother told me off about that.

"The colts that live here are good creatures," she said, "but they will grow up to be common cart horses. They haven't learned their manners."

I didn't understand what she meant, at first.

"You have been well-bred," continued Mother. "Your father was a very well-respected horse. And your grandfather won races at Newmarket, the most famous racecourse in the world. Your grandmother was the gentlest of animals. And as for me, I'm sure you've never seen me kick or bite another horse."

I hadn't.

"So don't learn bad habits from the colts," she warned. "Remember to always work without complaining. Lift your feet up well when you trot. And never kick or bite."

I never forgot my mother's advice. She was a beautiful and clever old horse. Farmer Gray was very fond of her. Her name was Duchess but he called her Pet.

Our master was a kind man. We had all the food and shelter we needed. He spoke to us as if we were his children. We were all fond of him and my mother loved him very much.

When she saw him at the gate, she would neigh with joy and trot over to him.

He'd stroke her nose and say, "Well, old Pet, how is your little Stormy?"

That was what he called me when I was young.

I had a shiny black coat with three white patches on it. My right foot was all white. People said I looked like I was wearing a white sock. I also had a white patch of hair on my back and another shaped like a star on my forehead.

Of all Farmer Gray's horses, we were his

We were his favorites.

favorites. Mother always pulled him to market in a little cart.

Yes, my earliest years were very pleasant. Everything was happiness and fun. I especially loved it when Flora and Jessie, the two young daughters of Squire Gordon, came to play with us.

They had an older brother called George. And it was something that happened to him, that taught me my first lesson about how cruel life could be.

I will never forget the day it all happened.

Chapter 2
The Hunt

It was springtime. The other colts and I were at the bottom of the meadow when we heard dogs crying out. The oldest colt raised his head and pricked up his ears. "It's the hounds!" he said.

He galloped up to the top the meadow. We followed. From there, we could see for miles and miles.

My mother was with us. "They are chasing a fox," she said. "If they come this way, we'll see the hunt."

And soon the dogs, yelping wildly, were tearing across the fields below us.

I saw the fox. It was racing towards our meadow.

The dogs were getting closer all the time. Behind them came men and women on horses, galloping as fast as they could.

"Here come the hunters," said Mother.

The leading hunter was dressed in a dark

The Hunt

"It's the hounds!"

green jacket. He was blowing a hunting horn. The hounds were howling "yo! yo! o! o!" at the top of their voices.

The riders saw the fox too and cried out: "Tally-ho!" to urge everyone to hurry on.

The fox dived under the hedge at the bottom of the valley, raced down the bank and leapt into the stream. It quickly swam across and hurried up the slope towards our meadow.

The riders didn't hesitate. The leading horses leapt the hedge and skidded down the bank into the stream. The splashing water sparkled in the bright morning sunlight.

Then they were off again, racing up the hill after the fox.

At that moment, something caught my eye. I saw one of the riders at the rear of the hunt reach the hedge. It was Squire Gordon's son George and he was riding my brother, a beautiful and bold horse called Rob Roy.

The horse seemed to lose his footing as it started to jump the hedge. I watched Rob Roy rise into the air, with George Gordon sitting tall in the saddle.

Instinct told me something was wrong. Rob Roy was not high enough to clear the hedge. His front feet hit the top.

The Hunt

George Gordon was flung into the air and tumbled to the ground. After that, he didn't move. Rob Roy somersaulted onto the bank below and rolled into the stream.

Meanwhile, the fox was in trouble. With the dogs at its heels, it ran into a yard surrounded by a high wall. There was no escape. I didn't see what happened, but I heard a terrible chorus of wild cries as the dogs closed in. Then I heard a single shriek.

One of the huntsmen rode up and called off the dogs. He waved gleefully at the other riders. They all seemed pleased that the fox had been caught.

I looked back to the stream. My brother was still lying where he had fallen. He was groaning and trying to get up, but he couldn't.

My mother knew immediately what had happened. She had seen it happen before, to other horses.

"Rob Roy's leg is broken," she said, sadly. "He won't get up again."

Other riders now gathered around George Gordon. They were looking very serious. He still wasn't moving. Someone lifted up his head. Then it slumped back to the ground. George Gordon was dead.

He was flung into the air.

There was no noise now. Even the dogs fell silent.

"I can never understand why people like hunting," said my mother. "So many of them get hurt when they jump over hedges and streams. A lot of horses also get hurt . . . and all for a fox. But then, what do we horses know? Perhaps people have their own reasons for wanting to hunt, despite hurting themselves, ruining good horses and tearing up the fields."

Four men picked up George Gordon's body and carried it to the farmhouse.

A vet walked down to the stream to look at Rob Roy, who was still struggling to get up. I saw the man shake his head.

He went back up to the farmhouse and quickly returned with a gun. My mother nudged me away and we went down to the bottom of the meadow.

Moments later, my brother had been put out of his misery.

My mother was most upset, and so was I.

A few days later the church bells rang out as a black carriage, pulled by two black horses, took George Gordon's body to be buried.

He would never ride again. What they did with Rob Roy, I never found out.

But both deaths were the price man and

horse paid, just for chasing one little fox.

Chapter 3
School

The day of the hunt was a first reminder that my life was not to be one long, happy frolic in the meadow. I was growing up.

It was time to be taught how to be a working horse, so I could pull carts and carriages and be ridden by my master. This training was called "breaking in" a horse.

My training started with lessons on how to wear a saddle, bridle, reins, and a nasty thing called a bit.

The bridle is made of straps that go around the head, under the throat and chin, and around the nose.

At first, I hated the bridle. But the bit was worse. Those who have never had a bit in their mouths cannot imagine how horrible it feels.

The bit is a piece of metal, as thick as a man's finger. It is attached to the bridle and reins, and is pushed into a horse's mouth. Then it is used by the rider or coach driver to guide the horse.

When the rider or driver pulls on the reins the horse must stop, or turn in the direction they are pulling him. If he does not, the bit hurts his mouth.

I thought the bit was a dreadful thing. But I knew my mother always wore a bit and bridle, and Farmer Gray was as kind as he could be. So I soon got used to wearing them.

The next part of my training was to learn to let people ride me. Farmer Gray slipped a saddle onto my back and secured it with some straps. Then he got into the saddle and rode me around the meadow.

I felt very odd for a while. But I must say that I also felt very proud to be carrying my master.

Then I was taken to the blacksmith, to have my shoes fitted. These were pieces of iron made to fit the shape of my feet. Each one was nailed to my hooves. Surprisingly, that didn't hurt at all.

Lastly, I was trained to wear a special harness. This was to help me pull carts and carriages.

All these things were very strange at first. But it was all part of growing up. I was only a young horse and had much to learn.

*

Learning to let people ride me.

One day I was moved to another meadow, on a neighboring farm. Here I was put in amongst a large herd of cows. I hadn't been there long when I heard a very strange sound. I turned around to see a great machine on rails hurtle past me. It was belching clouds of smoke from a chimney.

I was so frightened that I galloped to the other side of the meadow and watched the strange thing thunder away into the distance. The cows didn't even bother to move. They had seen it many times.

How was I to know what it was? I had never seen a locomotive before.

I soon got used to seeing locomotives pass the meadow and took no notice of them. Now, thanks to good Farmer Gray's care, I am fearless at railway stations. He knew the very best ways to train a young horse.

My mother also helped with my early training. We were often harnessed together to pull my master in a cart.

On those days, my mother gave me lots of advice. The most important thing she told me was that I should always obey my master, and do what he wanted.

"The better you behave, the better you'll be

I had never seen a locomotive before.

19

treated," she used to say.

But she also warned me that not all masters were like Farmer Gray.

"There are many different sorts of people," she said, "and they are not all good, kindly people like our master. There are bad, cruel people who should never be allowed to keep a horse or a dog."

My mother also told me that there were foolish, ignorant owners who ruined their horses because they did not take the trouble to learn how to care for them. These owners were just as bad as cruel owners, she said.

"I hope that you find a good master when you leave here," she added. "But a horse never knows who might buy him. It's all a matter of chance. All I can advise is that you always do your best and keep up your good name."

Chapter 4
A New Owner

When I was four years old, Squire Gordon came down to the meadow with Farmer Gray, to look at me.

The Squire examined my eyes and mouth, and my legs. Then he asked a stable boy to walk, trot and gallop me in front of him.

The Squire seemed to like me.

"He'll be a good horse," he said.

That was the day I learned that Squire Gordon was to be my new owner.

"Goodbye, Stormy," said Farmer Gray. "Be a good horse and always do your best. I shall miss you."

I put my nose in his hand and he patted me gently. I was sad to be leaving my first home.

The Squire lived in a big hall at a place called Birtwick Park. I was walked from the farm to Birtwick Park, and led into a large stable.

The stable was very clean, with lots of fresh

Leaving my first home.

straw covering the floor. There I was given a feed of oats and hay.

I wasn't alone. The stable was split into several stalls, with a wooden fence separating each one.

In the stall beside mine stood a fat, gray pony with a thick mane and tail, a pretty head and a pert nose.

I poked my head over the wooden fence that separated us. "And who are you?" I asked.

"My name is Merrylegs," he answered. "I am ridden by the young ladies, Miss Flora and Miss Jessie. And sometimes the Squire's wife rides out with me. Are you going to live here?"

"Yes," I answered.

"I hope you don't bite," said Merrylegs.

Just then, another horse in a stall at the back of the stable looked over at me. She was a tall chestnut mare and looked rather ill-tempered.

"So you are the horse that has turned me out of my own stall," she said, sharply. "I used to live where you are now. It's a fine thing for a colt like you to turn a lady out of her home."

"I beg your pardon. I have turned no one out of their home," I replied. "I was put in here by a groom."

"Say what you like," she answered, rudely.

With that, she lay down again. Later, Merrylegs told me her name was Ginger. "She bites and that is why she was moved to the back of the stable," he explained. "She frightened Miss Flora and Miss Jessie."

That night, Merrylegs told me that I was very lucky to belong to the Squire.

"There's not a better place for a horse to be than here," he said. "John Manly is the kindest groom around and James, the stable boy, makes

"My name is Merrylegs."

sure we are never short of food. And the Squire never uses a whip, as long as we horses behave ourselves."

The following day I met John Manly. He was to be my next teacher.

Chapter 5
A New Name

John Manly was Squire Gordon's head groom and coachman. He lived in the cottage beside the stables with his wife and baby.

On the first morning, he took me out riding. We met the Squire on the way back to the stables.

"What do you think of the new horse?" asked the Squire.

"First rate," answered John. "He's as nimble as a deer and has a fine spirit. And the slightest touch on the reins will guide him."

The next day the Squire took me out. I remembered my mother's advice and was determined to do exactly what he wanted of me.

Like John Manly, he was a very good and gentle rider. When we got back, his wife was waiting at the stables.

"How do you like him?" she asked her husband.

"You couldn't find a nicer horse," answered

A New Name

"How do you like him?"

the Squire. "But we'd better find a name for him now."

"How about calling him Ebony? He's so beautifully black," suggested Mrs. Gordon.

The Squire didn't like the name. So she said they could call him Blackbird, after her uncle's old horse.

"No," said the Squire. "This horse is much more handsome than Blackbird ever was."

"Yes, he's quite a beauty," said Mrs. Gordon. "He's got such a sweet-tempered face and very intelligent looks. Let's call him Black Beauty!"

"Black Beauty. That says it all," said the Squire. "That will be his name."

John Manly seemed very proud of me. And I grew very fond of him. He was so gentle and kind. When he cleaned me, he knew all the tender places that tickled me. And when he brushed my head, he went as carefully over my eyes as if they were his own.

And young James was just as nice.

A few days after my arrival, I had to help Ginger pull the Squire's carriage. I wondered how the two of us would get on together. But Ginger was a good worker and pulled as hard as me. We worked well as partners in harness.

As for Merrylegs, he and I soon became

close friends. He was such a cheerful, plucky little fellow.

All in all, I was very happy at Birtwick Park. But there were things I missed. I was sorry to be separated from my mother. And I also greatly missed the freedom of my younger days.

For the first few years of my life, I had been free to wander around my own meadow. I had been used to galloping wild, with my head held high and my tail tossing in the air. I could splash in the pond, chase the other colts and race around the shady trees.

Now I was shut in my stable for much of the time, unless I was needed to do a job.

I couldn't really complain, because that is the life of a horse. But I was a young horse, full of life and spirit, and John Manly understood this. When we were out exercising, he would always try to find time to give me a good gallop.

Sometimes he turned us out in the old orchard for a few hours. We could gallop, lie down, roll over on our backs and nibble the sweet grass.

It was on one of those days that Ginger and I stood beneath a chestnut tree and had a long talk. She told me that not all horses had as happy a young life as I'd had.

We stood beneath the chestnut tree.

Chapter 6
Ginger's Sad Story

"I never had anyone, horse or man, who was kind to me when I was young," Ginger began, as we stood in the shade. "I was taken away from my mother as soon as I was weaned and sent to live with a group of colts. None of them cared for me. I had no kind master like yours to look after me. My master never had a good word for me."

Ginger told me how a path ran through the meadow she lived in, when she was young. Boys used to walk down it and throw stones at her.

Then she explained how cruelly she had been trained.

"They came for me in the field one day. One person grabbed my head and another caught me by the nose. He held it so tightly that I couldn't breathe. Then they forced on a bridle and pushed the bit into my mouth."

Ginger said that she had been dragged away

with a lead by one man, while another followed behind, whipping her on.

"I was ridden by my master's son," she continued, "and he boasted he could tame any horse. There was no kindness about him. He had a hard voice, a hard eye and a very hard hand. All he wanted to do was to ride the spirit out of me. He just saw me as horse flesh."

Ginger said she had been badly hurt by the bit.

"I'm as proud a horse as you," she went on, "and one day, the bit was hurting my mouth so much that I reared up in anger. The boy just dug his spurs into my sides and whipped me cruelly. It was too much. I reared up again and threw him off my back."

"What happened then?" I asked.

"My owners didn't want me any more after that. I was sold to a gentleman in London. My new owner was wealthy and had fashionable friends."

It was then that Ginger told me about a cruel rein used by wealthy owners, who wanted their horses to keep up with the fashions of the day.

"It's called a bearing rein," said Ginger. "You won't have seen one yet, but it is very

Ginger's Sad Story

Ginger was cruelly trained.

painful. The rein pulls until your head is forced high into the air. And there you must keep it, until your work is over and your harness removed."

"Didn't your master worry about hurting you?" I asked.

"No," explained Ginger. "He just wanted his horses to look as fashionable as those of his friends. They all used those cruel bearing reins."

"How long did that go on for?" I asked.

"For ages. I got very angry. The special rein hurt my neck and sometimes I couldn't breathe properly. I started to kick up a fuss every time they came to put the rein on me. I tried to bite anyone who came near me. So they decided to get rid of me too. Soon after, I was sold to a country gentleman. He was a kind man but he had a cruel stable boy."

Ginger told me how the boy would hit her around the legs with the stable broom.

"One day, I bit him. That only made him angrier with me. He started hitting me around the head with his whip. And because of that I was sold again. That's how I came to be here."

I felt very sorry for Ginger but I didn't think she should have bitten the Squire's children,

"They all used those cruel bearing reins."

Miss Flora and Miss Jessie. So I asked her why she'd done it.

"I didn't mean to," Ginger replied. "But that was when I first arrived. I thought every person was cruel then. I know now that Flora and Jessie are really kind. I haven't snapped at them since and I won't again. They have shown me that some people can be kind."

John Manly, James the stable boy, the children and the Squire himself, had all seen how Ginger had become a better-behaved horse.

And they all knew why. It was because everyone had been kind to her.

Chapter 7
Merrylegs and Sir Oliver

Merrylegs was a horse that gave great pleasure to Miss Flora and Miss Jessie. But he also saw it as his job to train the children if they became too excitable.

One day I heard young James scolding Merrylegs.

"You behave yourself, you little rascal," he warned, "or you'll get into trouble."

Later, I asked Merrylegs what he had been doing.

"Oh!" he said, tossing his head cheerfully, "the children were misbehaving, so I decided to teach them a lesson. Three of them were sitting on my back and trying to make me gallop around the paddock. That was a dangerous thing to do. So I pitched them off."

"What!" I said, quite shocked. "You threw them off?"

"Only in a very gentle way," he answered. "They have to learn. And I am a good teacher.

I have to break them in, just like we were broken in."

Sir Oliver, another of the Squire's horses, was listening to our talk. At this point, he interrupted us. "Those young girls are little angels compared with the people who had me when I was young. Just look at my tail."

Sir Oliver's tail was very short.

"Did that happen in an accident?" I asked.

"Accident!" he snorted. "It was a cruel, cold-blooded act! My owners cut off the bottom half of my tail. The pain was terrible and lasted a long while. But the worst thing was that afterwards, I couldn't use my tail to swish away the flies. They really tormented me. Just imagine what it would be like if you couldn't brush off a fly that was biting you."

"Why did your owners do it?" I asked.

"For fashion," he answered. "In those days, every well-bred young horse had his tail shortened. They thought it made us look better."

"And it's fashion that makes some people use those horrible bearing reins," said Ginger.

"Of course," said Sir Oliver. "To my mind, fashion is one of the wickedest things in the world."

Sir Oliver was a gentle horse, but he could be a fiery old fellow when he felt like it.

"I decided to teach them a lesson."

I listened to what he said and started to understand how cruel some people could be.

"We are lucky," said Ginger, "that we have a good master and a kind groom, and stable boy."

Soon after, I saw an example of a bad owner.

John Manly and I were returning from town one morning when we saw Bill Bushby, a farmer's son, trying to force his pony to leap a high gate.

The pony refused to jump, despite being whipped. We saw Bill get off and give the pony a thrashing with his whip. Then he started kicking it.

The pony still refused to jump the gate.

When we reached the spot the pony put its head down and threw up its heels, kicking the boy into the air. Bill Bushby tumbled into the spiky hawthorn hedge.

With the reins dangling around its head, the pony set off home at a full gallop.

John laughed out aloud. "Serves you right!" he said.

Bill hardly dared move for fear of the sharp thorns sticking into him. "Help me!" he cried.

"It seems to me," John told him, "that you are in the right place! Maybe a thorn or two will teach you not to try and force a pony to jump a gate that is clearly too high for him."

With that, John told me to head for home. Back at the Hall, he told James that he remembered Bill from school.

"Bill used to bully boys younger than him," he recalled, "and he liked to catch flies, and pull off their wings. I gave him a box on the ears for that. But he never changed. Look how he behaved today."

Then John said that he thought cruelty was the mark of the devil.

"Help me!"

41

Chapter 8
The Storm

One day late in the autumn, Squire Gordon had to go to town on business. He was going to travel with John Manly in a small cart. I was to pull them.

It had been raining for several days. When we reached the wooden bridge over the river, close to the village of Birtwick, the water level was rising fast. Many of the surrounding meadows were already under water.

We passed through the village and two hours later, we reached the town. The Squire took quite a while to finish his business and we did not set off for home until late.

By the time we reached the wood near Birtwick, the rain was coming down in torrents and the wind was starting to howl. Huge tree branches were swaying about like twigs.

"I've never been out in such a dreadful storm," I heard the Squire say. "I'll be glad when we're out of this wood."

The Storm

The wind was starting to howl.

The words were hardly out of his mouth when there was a groan, a crack and a splitting sound. A great oak tree, torn out by it roots, crashed across the road right in front of us.

I was badly frightened. But I had been trained not to panic and run away. John quickly leapt off the cart and came to comfort me.

"That was a near thing," said the Squire.

"We can't get past the tree," said John, "we'll have to go back and take the other road."

So back we went and took the other road home. By the time we reached the bridge near Birtwick it was almost dark. But we could just see that the river had risen so high that a few inches of water now covered the middle of the bridge.

The Squire told John to drive on. A few inches of water was nothing to worry about, he said.

We were going a good pace. But the moment my feet touched the first part of the bridge, I came to a dead stop. I knew something was wrong.

"Go on, Beauty," said the Squire, giving me a touch with his whip.

I still didn't move.

"There's something wrong, sir," said John,

The Storm

I knew something was wrong.

leaping off the cart and trying to lead me forward on foot. "Beauty's worried about something."

Of course I could not tell him, but I knew very well that the bridge was not safe.

Just then, a man with a lantern appeared on the other side of the river. "Don't go a step further!" he shouted. "The bridge is broken in the middle. The flood has washed part of it away."

"You clever horse, Beauty," said John, turning me around and heading off to take the other bridge, further upstream. "You've saved our lives."

The Squire was very pleased with me. "If Beauty had not stopped," he said, "we would all have been in the river. The flood would have swept us to our deaths. We would have drowned."

On the way back, John and the Squire talked about how animals often saved their owners' lives.

"The water was hiding the missing part of that bridge," said John, "yet Beauty knew by instinct that something wasn't right. I wish we humans were as clever as horses can be."

At last we saw the distant lights of the Hall. The Squire's wife ran out to greet us.

"You're so late!" she said. "I thought you'd had an accident."

"We almost did," said the Squire, "but Beauty's wisdom and instinct saved us. But for him, we would have all been swept away at the bridge."

What a supper they gave me that night! I had bran, crushed beans and oats. John even made an extra thick bed of straw for me. I was glad of it, for I was very tired.

Chapter 9
Night in the Hotel Stable

A few weeks later, Ginger and I took the Squire to town again. This time James was driving. We were to stay at a local hotel.

We drove through an archway into the hotel yard. The Squire went in while James led us into the stables. There were several other horses already there.

James tied us up in our stalls and gave us our food, before going into the hotel for his own supper.

Later that evening another rider arrived. He was smoking a pipe. He climbed into the hayloft above our stalls and brought down some hay for his horse. Then he left.

James popped in a few minutes later, to check that we were settled for the night. Then he left us again, locking the stable door behind him.

I cannot say how long I had slept, or what time of night it was. But I woke up feeling very uncomfortable. It was dark and the air seemed thick and choking.

I heard Ginger coughing. The other horses were moving about restlessly.

I could hardly breathe. Then I heard a strange crackling sound, coming from the hayloft.

I did not know what it was but it scared me. I began to tremble all over.

At last I heard footsteps outside. The door was unlocked and a man burst into the stable with a lantern in his hand. Quickly, he began to untie the horses.

He tried to lead some of the horses out of the door. But he was frightened himself and that fear spread to us all. The first horse would not go with him. Nor would the second, or the third.

Then he came to me. But I was trembling so much I refused to move. The man saw it was hopeless. He ran to get help.

No doubt we were very foolish not to leave the stable when asked to, but danger seemed to be all around us. And there was nobody we knew to trust.

The fresh air that came through the door made it easier to breathe. But it seemed to make the crackling sound more violent.

Someone cried out, "Fire!"

The air seemed thick and choking.

Chapter 10
Fire!

I saw red flames licking around the hayloft trapdoor. The next thing I heard was James' calm voice.

"Come on, my beauties," he said, "it's time you were out of here!"

He came to me first. He took the scarf off his neck and tied it lightly over my eyes to calm me down. Then he gently led me outside to safety.

Once we were safe in the yard, James took the scarf from my eyes.

"Here, somebody!" he shouted. "Take this horse while I go back for the other."

A man stepped forward and held me, as James darted back into the stable. I made a loud whinny to let Ginger know that I was already outside, and safe.

There was such confusion in the yard. Horses were running this way and that. Servants were hauling carriages and carts away from the blaze. I kept my eyes fixed on the

He led me outside to safety.

stable door, from where the smoke was pouring out thicker than ever.

On the other side of the yard, hotel windows were opened and people were shouting out all sorts of things. I heard the Squire's voice call out.

"James? Are you there, James?"

Then I saw James coming through the smoke, leading Ginger with him. Ginger was coughing violently. I gave a loud, joyful neigh to see her.

The Squire soon appeared in the yard.

"Brave lad," he said, putting his arm around James. "Are you hurt?"

James shook his head. He still couldn't speak for the smoke.

Just then, I heard the sound of galloping horses and rumbling wheels.

"It's the fire engine! The fire engine!" cried the onlookers. "Stand back! Make way for the fire engine!"

Two horses dashed into the yard, pulling the fire engine behind them. The firemen leapt off the machine, just as flames burst through the roof of the stable.

We left the hotel as fast as we could. We found another hotel on the other side of the market place. Ginger and I were taken into the stable and given some hay.

The next morning we heard James say that the fire had been caused by the man who had arrived late. He had left his burning pipe in the hayloft.

The worst news of all was that two horses had failed to get out. They had died in the dreadful fire.

Ginger told me afterwards that she was very grateful I had whinnied to let her know I was outside and safe.

"Make way for the fire engine!"

54

She said she was so frightened by the fire that she might never have come out, even with James leading her.

It wasn't long after the fire that James left us to go to work as head groom and coachman at another big hall nearby.

His place was taken by Joe Green, from the village of Birtwick. He was only fourteen years old.

Joe was not experienced in looking after horses. But he was a good, honest farmer's boy, and the Squire wanted to give him a chance to learn.

It was a decision that could have cost me my life.

Chapter 11
Ride for Your Life!

A few days after James left, I was woken by John Manly rushing into my stable.

"Wake up, Beauty," he said. "There's work to be done."

He had my saddle and bridle on before I knew it. Then he leapt onto my back and galloped across to the Hall door. The Squire was standing there with a lantern in his hand.

"Now, John," he said, "you must ride for your life. It's your mistress. She's terribly ill and there's not a moment to lose. Go and get the doctor. Tell him it's urgent!"

"Come on, Beauty," cried John. "Let's see how fast you can run!"

We dashed through the park, into the village and down the hill, until we reached the main road. A long straight section stretched ahead of us.

"Go like the wind!" shouted John.

He didn't need a whip or spurs to encourage

"Go like the wind!"

me. I galloped for the next two miles. I don't believe my grandfather, who won at Newmarket races, could have gone faster.

The air was frosty and the moon was out. We raced through one more village, climbed another hill, clattered over an old wooden bridge and finally reached the town.

It was three o'clock in the morning by the time John knocked on Doctor White's door.

A window opened and Doctor White, wearing his nightcap, put out his head. "What do you want, John?"

"Mrs. Gordon is very ill," said John, "The Squire wants you to come at once. He thinks she'll die."

The doctor scratched his head. "I've got a problem," he said. "My horse is lame and I can't take him out."

"Then take Black Beauty," said John. "He's galloped all the way here, but he's got the biggest heart I know. He'll take you."

John leapt off and a few moments later the doctor came out, and got into the saddle.

I turned and galloped away.

The doctor was a heavier man than John and he wasn't such a good rider. But I did my best. By the time we reached the village again

I was almost out of breath.

"Come on, boy," said the doctor. "We're nearly there now."

I raced into the park and pulled up outside the front door of the Hall.

The doctor hurried into the house while young Joe Green led me back to the stable.

I was exhausted. I could do nothing but stand and pant for a while. My legs were shaking and there wasn't a dry hair on my body. Sweat was running down my sides.

Poor Joe was so young and inexperienced that he did not know what to do. He should have put my horse blanket over me so that I would cool down slowly.

Instead, he just gave me a big pail of icy water and some hay. Then he left me.

Soon after, my shaking grew worse and I became deathly cold. My legs and chest ached terribly. I felt sore all over. How I wished for my warm blanket. And how I wished for John!

John had to walk all the way home. Hours later I heard his weary footsteps. I gave a low moan, for I was in great pain.

He hurried into the stable and saw immediately what the problem was. He covered me with three blankets and ran to the Hall for

I was exhausted.

some hot water. Then he made me some warm soup with oats. I ate it and then fell into a deep sleep.

I woke up late the next day. I had a fever and could hardly breathe.

The fever got worse over the next few days.

John nursed me night and day. He got up two or three times a night to come and see how I was.

"My poor Beauty," he said, "you saved your mistress's life. Yes, you did. You saved her. Now you are close to death."

John told the Squire that he had never seen a horse go as fast as I had done that night. He said it was as if I knew how important it was to get to the doctor quickly.

Of course I knew that! I also knew that I was now very sick.

Chapter 12
Joe's Good Deed

The vet came to see me every day. And one
morning, young Joe Green's father came to see
how I was.

He was very upset because Joe was broken-
hearted at what had happened. Joe knew I was
ill because he hadn't looked after me properly
after my exhausting gallop.

"I wish you'd have a word with Joe," he said
to John Manly. "The boy is so upset. He knows
it was his fault and he blames himself for everything. He was just too young to know what to
do. If Beauty dies I don't think he'll ever be the
same again. He's not a bad boy."

"Oh, I know he's not," said John. "It would
break my heart too, if Beauty died. That horse
is the pride of my heart and a real favorite of
the Squire's. If Beauty is better in the morning
I will have a word with Joe."

As it happened, I was much better in the
morning. So kindly John did have a word with

"It would break my heart too, if Beauty died."

young Joe. The boy had learned his lesson and never made another mistake. John came to trust him completely.

*

After a few weeks' rest I was completely recovered. Then Joe was allowed to ride me for the first time. John wanted Joe to deliver a message to a man who lived some three miles away from the Hall.

Joe saddled me and rode me very carefully all the way there. On the way back, we came upon a cart heavily loaded with bricks. It was being pulled by two horses and was now stuck in some deep, muddy cart tracks.

The driver was flogging both horses unmercifully with his whip. The horses were doing their best to pull the cart, but they couldn't move it. Sweat was streaming from their sides and every muscle was straining.

"Hold hard!" cried Joe. "Don't go flogging the horses like that. Those wheels are really stuck fast."

But the man carried on whipping the horses. "Mind your own business, young 'un!" he shouted.

Joe didn't bother to argue with the man but rode me straight to the home of Mr. Clay, the man who owned the brickyard.

He told Mr. Clay how the man had been treating the horses. And Mr. Clay thanked Joe for the information.

"I shall take him to the magistrate for cruelty," he said.

When we got back to the Hall, John Manly praised Joe for what he had done. "Many folk

"Don't go flogging the horses like that."

would have just passed on by without doing anything," he said. "You made it your business to help those horses. You did right, my boy."

A few days later I heard that Joe had gone to court to give evidence to the magistrate. And on that day the magistrate was Squire Gordon himself. He thanked Joe for reporting the cruelty and sent the man to prison for a week.

Chapter 13
Sad Days

I had now lived at Birtwick Park for three years. But changes were coming.

The Squire's wife never fully recovered from the illness that called for my lightning ride to the doctor. The doctor often came to the Hall now.

It was he who decided that the mistress must go and live in a warmer country. He was sure that living in a country with hot sunshine and warm air would cure her.

The Squire looked very worried. He had to make plans to leave the Hall and go abroad.

Everyone was sorry to hear the news. John went about his work silent and sad. Joe's happy morning whistle was heard no more.

The Squire's two daughters, Miss Flora and Miss Jessie, were the first to leave. They came to the stable in tears. They hugged poor Merrylegs like an old friend. Ginger and I got a kiss on the nose too.

We soon learned what was to happen to us.

Ginger and I had been sold to the Squire's friend, Lord White.

Merrylegs was to be given to the church minister, Mr. Blomefield, who had two sons. Joe was to go with Merrylegs and also do odd jobs for the minister.

John Manly quickly found a position as head groom to another squire in the area.

And so, the last day came. All the luggage had been sent on ahead. Only the Squire, his wife and some of the servants were left.

Ginger and I brought the carriage up to the front door for the last time. John Manly drove us, with Joe beside him. The door opened and the Squire came out, carrying his wife in his arms.

The servants behind them were all in tears.

"Goodbye to you all," said the Squire. "I'll never forget any of you."

Once in the carriage, he gave one last wave and then told John to drive on.

We trotted through the park and into the village. People were standing sadly at their doors to wave goodbye to a kind master.

When we reached the station, the Squire hugged both Ginger and I. Even Mrs. Gordon

And so, the last day came.

managed to stroke my nose. There were tears in her eyes.

"Goodbye, Beauty," the Squire said, sadly. "Goodbye, Ginger."

Then they were gone. I heard the train pull into the station. Doors slammed and a whistle blew loudly. Then the train glided away, leaving behind clouds of white smoke and some very heavy hearts.

"We'll never see the mistress again," said John. "Never!"

He took the reins and we drove slowly on to our new lives.

Chapter 14
Another New Home

The next morning after breakfast, Joe and Merrylegs left for Mr. Blomefield's house. Merrylegs neighed sadly to us as he trotted away.

John saddled Ginger and put me on a leading rein. Then he took us the fifteen miles to where Lord White lived. Lord White had a fine house and lots of stables. We were met by York, the coachman and head groom.

York was a middle-aged man and his voice said at once that he expected to be obeyed. He glanced at Ginger and I briefly, and called a stable boy to see us into the stable.

We were taken to a light, airy stable and placed in stalls beside each other. The boy rubbed us down and fed us.

Later, John and York came to see us. "The horses look fine," said York. "Do they have any habits you want to tell me about?"

"No. I don't believe there is a finer pair of horses in the country," replied John. "But

Ginger is worth watching. She was badly treated as a youngster. She was quite snappy when she first came to us. But she's been nothing but good since then. Treated well, you'll not find a better or more willing horse."

They were leaving the stable when John stopped. "There is one thing I must mention," he said, seriously. "We have never used the cruel bearing rein on either of the horses."

York answered him quickly. "If they are to stay here, they must wear the bearing rein. His Lordship is very kind to all his horses, but her Ladyship, she's another thing altogether. She insists that her horses must wear the bearing rein. She is determined to be seen doing the fashionable thing, however much it hurts them."

"I am very sorry to hear it," said John. "I can only warn you to be careful with Ginger if she is hurt with the bearing rein."

York promised he would do all he could to make our lives as comfortable as possible.

John came round to pat and speak to us for the last time. His voice was breaking with sadness. I held my face close to his. He stroked my nose. And then he was gone.

The next day, Lord White came with York to look at us.

Another New Home

"The horses look fine."

"If Ginger was treated badly as a youngster," said his Lordship, "be gentle when you first put the bearing rein on."

"Aye, sir," said York, "I'll speak to her ladyship about it."

That afternoon, York put bearing reins on both Ginger and I. With our heads forced high into the air by the reins, we pulled a smart carriage around to the front door of the house.

We saw a woman appear at the front door. She was tall and proud-looking. She came down the steps, took a brief glance at Ginger and I and got into the carriage without a word.

We drove her Ladyship for a few miles, before returning home. The bearing rein did pull my head quite high but it wasn't too uncomfortable.

I felt anxious for Ginger. I though she might become awkward with the rein on. But she didn't seem too upset.

The following day we were brought to the front door again. Her Ladyship came down the steps, stopped and looked up.

"York," she said, angrily, "you must get those horses' heads higher. They are not fit to be seen in fashionable society. Tighten the bearing rein!"

We saw a woman appear at the front door.

York got down. "I beg your pardon, my lady, but his Lordship said it would be safer to get them used to the bearing rein slowly. But if your Ladyship pleases, I can make them raise their heads a little more."

"Do so, then," she answered, coldly.

York came around and tightened the reins.

That day we had to climb a steep hill. It was then that I began to understand what I had heard about the bearing rein. Now I had to pull with my head right up in the air. It put a terrible strain on my back and legs. And I couldn't breathe properly any more.

When we got back, Ginger spoke to me. "If that bearing rein gets any tighter, her Ladyship had better watch out. I won't stand for it!"

Chapter 15
Disaster

Day by day, our bearing reins became tighter. Instead of looking forward to a run out, now we began to dread it.

My mouth was bruised and my throat was very sore. Ginger was worse. Her neck had become so stiff that she couldn't sleep at night.

One summer evening, her Ladyship stormed down the hall steps with two footmen at her side. She was wearing a beautiful dress of the finest silk.

"York!" she snapped. "We are going to the Duchess's garden party, so tighten up those reins! I want those horses' heads right up. There will be no more of this gentle tightening. I have humored those animals long enough!"

York came to me first, while the stable boy held Ginger. He drew my head back and fixed the rein so tight that it was intolerable. Then he went to Ginger, who was already angrily jerking her head up and down.

She knew what was about to happen.

The moment York took hold of the rein, Ginger reared up on her hind legs, hitting him on the nose and knocking his hat off. The rein then caught around the stable boy's leg and he was knocked to the ground.

Ginger continued plunging, rearing and kicking in the panic that followed. She finally tripped over a part of the harness and fell down, hitting me hard on the side as she did so.

There is no knowing what damage Ginger might have done if York hadn't sat down on her head to stop her from struggling.

"Cut the harness!" he shouted. "Get the black horse out! Free the carriage!"

One of the footmen ran into the house for a knife. The stable boy finally freed himself and then me. He led me back to my box in the stable and left me with my bearing rein still attached to the harness.

I was sore and angry. Whatever I did, I could not bring my head down. I was so miserable that I felt like kicking the first person that came near me.

A little later, Ginger was led in by the stable boy. She was badly knocked about and bruised.

York followed her in and freed both our

Ginger reared up on her hind legs.

bearing reins. "Confound those reins," he said to himself, angrily. "I knew they would cause trouble with these two. His Lordship won't be happy. What can I do? If he can't tell his wife not to use the bearing reins, how can I?"

His Lordship was troubled when he found out what had happened. He blamed York for not standing up to her Ladyship. "Didn't you warn her what might happen with Ginger?" he asked.

"I had to obey her orders, my lord," replied York. "I don't think she would have listened to me."

His Lordship nodded in understanding.

Ginger never pulled the carriage again after that. One of his Lordship's younger sons decided to ride her for hunting instead.

As for me, they still used me with the carriage and I had a new partner, called Max. He had always been used to the tight rein and I asked him how he coped with it.

"I bear it because I must," he said, "but it will shorten my life for sure. And yours too, if you have to stick with it."

I asked him whether he thought Lord White knew how bad the bearing rein was for us horses.

They still used me in the carriage.

"I can't say, but the horse dealers and the vets know it well. They ignore it because the fashionable people who use the bearing rein are also the richest."

"What happens to horses that wear a bearing rein for a long time?" I asked.

"They get worn out with the head having to be constantly stretched high in the air. They end up getting diseased in the neck and back. They get breathing problems. Then their owners sell them and get another horse."

I felt so alone now. I always had friends in my old home, and I was always well treated.

Now I felt that all I had to look forward to was a life of pain and suffering.

Chapter 16
Another Accident

Early in the spring, his Lordship took his wife to London for a holiday.

But their daughter, Lady Anne, remained at home.

Lady Anne loved to take me out for a ride. She was a perfect horsewoman, and as happy and gentle as she was beautiful.

She had a cousin called David, who regularly visited. They would often ride out together. Lady Anne always rode me and David had Lizzie, a bright bay mare. Lizzie was a very well-bred horse and a favorite of the men who came to stay.

One day David suggested to Lady Anne that they swap horses for a change. He did warn her that Lizzie could be very lively.

"Don't worry," she laughed, "I have been riding since I was baby."

They rode us out to the edge of a village. We were passing a field full of carthorses and playful colts when the trouble started.

Lizzie panicked.

The horses in the field suddenly saw us and galloped over. Lizzie panicked. She reared up, nearly throwing Lady Anne off, and then galloped down the road. By the time we caught our breath, Lizzie and Lady Anne were around the corner and out of sight

David and I gave chase. Near the village, we caught sight of the pair. Lady Anne was still in the saddle and she was pulling back on the reins as hard as she could. Then they vanished around another corner.

When we saw them again, Lady Anne's hat was gone and her long brown hair was streaming out behind her. By this time, I don't think she had hold of the reins at all.

Up ahead, I saw a wide ditch. I was sure this would stop Lizzie. But no, Lizzie didn't hesitate. She leapt.

I saw her land, stumble and then fall.

I raced on, leapt the ditch and pulled up beside Lizzie and Lady Anne. Lizzie had struggled to her feet, but my poor young mistress lay face down and unmoving.

David knelt down beside Lady Anne. Her face was very pale and her eyes were closed. He looked around for someone to help him.

Two men, who had been working in a nearby

field, were already on their way across.

When the first man reached the scene, David told him to ride me to the doctor's house. "Tell him to come here instantly. Then ride back to the house and tell them what has happened."

The man scrambled into my saddle, and with a "Gee up!" I galloped away.

It didn't take us long to find the doctor and take the news back home.

Lady Anne did recover but she and her cousin never swapped horses again. She always rode me after that.

Her face was very pale.

Chapter 17
Reuben Smith

While York was in London with his Lordship, the under-coachman, Reuben Smith, was left in charge of the stables.

Reuben was very kind and gentle with horses. He could look after them as well as anyone. He was a wonderful rider too.

Everybody liked Reuben; certainly the horses did. But he had one great fault – a love of strong drink.

Once he had been sent to bring some of the family home from a big dance. But he was so drunk that he could not hold the reins. Someone else had to drive the carriage home.

The Earl immediately dismissed Reuben from his job. But later he took pity on the man and gave him his job back, on the promise that he would never drink another drop of alcohol.

Reuben kept to his promise so well that York felt he could be trusted to do his job while he was away.

One day, Lady Anne's cousin David had to return to London. Reuben and I drove him to town, to catch a train.

At the station, David put some money in Reuben's hand and thanked him for his trouble. Reuben was very pleased and whistled happily as we drove off.

Later, he left me in the stables at the White Lion Inn and disappeared into the inn. It was already dark when he returned. He was drunk, having clearly spent all the money that David had given him.

It was then that someone pointed out that one of my shoes had a nail missing.

"Never mind that," said Reuben. "It'll be all right until we get home. We're leaving the carriage here for repairs, anyway. I'll be riding him home."

I knew a loose nail could be dangerous and thought it was very unlike Reuben not to make sure I was all right before traveling anywhere.

I saw the landlord of the inn come to the door and call out to Reuben. "You've had a lot of whisky," he warned. "You be careful on the way home."

Reuben ignored the man, saddled me up and clambered into the saddle with great difficulty.

Everybody liked Reuben.

He cut me with his whip and sent me on my way at a gallop.

We were hardly out of town when my damaged shoe was ripped off by some large stones. Reuben was so drunk that he didn't notice when I suddenly stumbled. Instead, he just whipped me even harder.

We reached a piece of road that had just been repaired. It was covered in loose, sharp stones. In no time at all, they cut my shoeless hoof to pieces. It was split right down to the quick.

The pain was too great. I stumbled again and crashed violently to my knees. The fall threw Reuben off the saddle and over my head.

I struggled to my feet and limped to the side of the road. I knew that I had been badly hurt.

The moon had just risen and I could see Reuben lying a few yards away. He made a small movement and I heard a groan. Then all was silent.

I could have groaned too, for I was in great pain. But horses are used to bearing pain in silence. I made no sound. I just stood there and listened.

It was a warm May evening. A brown owl flitted over the hedge. It made me think of summer nights long ago, when I used to lie

My damaged shoe was ripped off.

beside my mother in the lovely meadow at Farmer Gray's.

It was nearly midnight when I finally heard someone approaching. As the sound came nearer and nearer, I was sure I recognized Ginger's steps.

I neighed loudly and was overjoyed to hear Ginger's answering call. She was pulling a cart with two of Lord White's men aboard. They had been sent to search for Reuben and I.

One of the men knelt down beside Reuben. He took hold of his hand and then spoke. "He's dead."

Chapter 18
A Sad Farewell

Nobody blamed me for Reuben's death. The shoe that had fallen from my hoof was quickly found. And people at the inn told of how drunk Reuben had been when he left that night.

However, my knees were badly damaged. Nobody was sure if my injuries would ever heal properly. The vet said I might never work again.

I was turned out into the meadow to rest and to see if I would recover.

I soon felt very lonely. I missed Ginger terribly. I often neighed when I heard horses' hooves passing on the road, but I seldom got an answer.

Then one morning the gate opened, and who should come into the meadow but dear old Ginger! A groom slipped off her bridle and left her there. With a joyful whinny, I trotted up to her.

Ginger brought me sad news. George, his Lordship's youngest son, was a hard rider. He had pushed her to the limit. She was coughing and limping.

"They've put me in this meadow to rest," she explained. "But I think I've been ruined forever."

Ginger told me how she had been taken to the races, just the day before. George was determined to ride her.

A groom had warned George that Ginger wasn't fit to run. She had a strained muscle in one of her back legs. But George, a tall and heavy young man, insisted she would be fine.

Poor Ginger ran her heart out for George. But all she got in return was a serious cough and a painful leg injury.

"So here we both are," she said, "ruined in the prime of our youth and strength – you by a drunkard and me by a fool who should have known better. It is hard to take."

I knew that Ginger spoke the truth. But at least we now had the joy of each other's company.

We did not gallop about the meadow as we once had, but we used to feed and lie down together. We also stood under the shady trees on hot days with our heads close together.

And so we passed the time until Lord White returned.

With a joyful whinny, I trotted up to her.

We saw his Lordship come into the meadow with York. They must have been told about our bad luck, because they came over and examined us very carefully.

They were both very angry.

"These horses have been ruined!" exclaimed Lord White, in disgust. "What am I to tell my old friend Squire Gordon, if he returns? I promised to look after them. But they are useless now."

His Lordship said he would keep Ginger for a year to see if she recovered. But for me, there was no hope.

"Black Beauty will have to be sold," he said. "Those knees will never mend properly and he will always have scars. Perhaps we can find someone who will take him in."

York said he knew of a man who might take me for a low price. "He runs a stable of horses for hire in the town of Bath," he said.

"You'd better arrange it, York," sighed his Lordship.

After this, they left us.

"They'll soon take you away," said Ginger, sadly. "I shall lose the only friend I have. Most likely we will never meet again. It's a hard world."

A Sad Farewell

How true were her words. A week later, York came into the meadow and put a bridle on me. There was no time to say a proper farewell to Ginger.

She neighed to me as I was led away, trotting anxiously along the hedge and calling to me for as long as she could hear the sound of my hooves.

I never expected to see her again.

"These horses have been ruined!"

Chapter 19
A New Job

York walked me to the nearest railway station where I was loaded onto a goods train for my journey to Bath.

I had never traveled on a train before. I found the puffing, rushing, swaying and rattling quite frightening at first. But I soon got used to it.

When I reached the end of my journey, I found myself in a fairly comfortable stable. I was well fed and cleaned. But the work was to be very different from what I was used to.

I became what is known as a "job horse". I was hired out to all sorts of people. Most of them knew nothing about riding or driving a horse.

Some held the reins so tight that the bit dug painfully into my mouth. Others drove with a very loose rein. This meant they had no control if some emergency happened.

Once I was hired to pull a small carriage. The driver took no notice of me at all. He spent all his time laughing and joking with the passengers. He didn't notice a thing, even when I got a sharp stone caught in my foot.

He drove me for a mile or more with the stone cutting into my hoof before he noticed I was limping.

"Now then, you old horse," he said, "don't pretend you're lame. We've got a long way to go yet."

Just then, a farmer came riding by. "I beg your pardon, sir," he said, "but that horse is lame. I think it must have got a stone in its foot. I'll have a look if you like."

"I doubt it's a stone," said my driver. "He's a hired horse. I think he must have been lame when I hired him."

The farmer got off his horse and lifted my leg. He quickly found the stone and pulled it out.

"Well, I never," said the driver. "I didn't know that horses could pick up stones like that!"

Then there were drivers who treated horses like machines.

They paid their money and then expected the horse to do everything else. Those people would never think of getting out of a carriage to walk up a steep hill. Oh, no, they had paid

"That horse is lame."

to ride and ride they would! Never mind the horse.

And when a horse tired, they took out the whip. "Come on, you lazy beast!" they'd cry.

Some drivers put the brake on the wheel of their carriage, to slow it down when it was traveling down a hill. Then they'd forget to free the brake at the bottom of the hill. So I would have to pull half way up the next slope with the wheels locked fast.

I would rather have gone twenty miles with a kind driver than one mile with one of those sorts of people. How I wished that every driver was as good as Farmer Gray, or John Manly, or Squire Gordon!

In the first few months that I worked as a horse for hire, I was quickly worn out with all the different jobs I had to do.

Once again, I was sold. This time, I was taken off to the local horse market.

Chapter 20
The Horse Market

People think horse markets are great fun. There are always lots of young horses to see, fresh from the country; dozens of shaggy little Welsh ponies and hundreds of different cart horses.

It's a big day out for people. Some come to buy a horse or pony, while others just want to look. But for horses, it is a very different matter.

When I arrived at the horse market I saw many horses like myself; handsome and well-bred creatures who had fallen on bad times.

Yet we were lucky when compared with the saddest of the horses brought to the market. They were broken by too much hard work. Their knees were so damaged that they could not walk straight and their hind legs were bent, and misshapen.

These horses had a tragic look. Their ears were laid back, their eyes were sunken and their heads hung low. It was as if they felt there

The Horse Market

The saddest of the horses brought to market.

was no more happiness to be had from life.

They were so thin that you could see their ribs. Some were covered with sores on their backs and hips. Who could tell how they came to be in that awful condition?

I was put in a stable with two or three other horses. Plenty of people came to look at us. But they always turned away from me when they saw the scars on my knees.

Some men did stop to examine me. They pulled open my mouth and looked in. Then they looked at my eyes, felt all the way down my legs and gave my skin a good pinch.

Some people were very rough. They treated me as if they were examining a piece of wood. Others were kinder. I judged those people by how they examined me.

There was one man who was very gentle and kind. I knew I would be happy if he bought me. He was not a man of high birth, nor one of the loud, flashy characters who imagined they were gentlemen.

I knew by the way he handled me that he was used to horses. He spoke gently and his gray eyes had a kindly, cheerful look to them. I reached out my head towards him and he stroked my face softly.

He stroked my face softly.

"Well, old chap," he said, "I think we might just suit each other."

He made an offer to the man who was selling me and the other horses.

"Done!" said the man. "And you can be sure you have a bargain here. He'll make a good working horse."

The money was paid and my new master led me away. He took me to the local inn, where he had a saddle and bridle ready.

He gave me a good feed of oats and soon after, we were on our way. Our destination was the city of London.

That evening we reached the edge of the big city. The gas lamps by the roadside had already been lit.

We finally turned off the main road and the man rode me up a side street. Half way up, we turned into a very narrow alley with rather poor-looking houses on either side.

My new owner pulled up in front of one of these and whistled.

The front door flew open and a young woman, followed by a little boy and girl, ran out.

"Open the stable door, Harry," said the man. "Bring a lantern, Mother."

The Horse Market

The next minute they were all standing around me in a small stable yard.

"Is he gentle, Father?" asked the little girl.

"Yes, Dolly," he answered, "as gentle as your own kitten. Come and pat him."

Dolly walked up to me and stroked my nose. How good it felt!

"I'll get him some food," said the woman, "while you rub him down."

I felt as though I was loved again. But I still didn't know what my next job was to be. The only thing I had heard at the market was that I might make a good cab horse.

Chapter 21
A London Cab Horse

I discovered that the man who had bought me was Jerry Barker, a London cab driver.

Jerry was married to Polly, a small woman with dark hair and eyes, and a happy, smiling face. Their son, Harry, was a kindly boy who looked a great deal like his father. He was twelve years old. His sister, Dolly, was just eight. She was a sweet-natured and cheerful little girl.

They all loved each other dearly. I never knew such a happy family.

Jerry had a cab of his own. I was to be his second horse. His other horse was called Captain.

Captain was a tall, proud animal with a snowy white coat. He was quite old but he must have been a splendid horse when he was young.

The morning after my arrival, I was groomed by Jerry and Harry. Polly and Dolly also came into the stable, with a slice of apple for me and a piece of bread for Captain.

Everyone made a great fuss of me.

Everyone made a great fuss of me.

It was wonderful to be treated so fondly again. I let them see that I wished to be a friendly horse.

Polly thought I was very handsome and too good to be just a cab horse, if it were not for my injured knees. They decided to call me Jack.

It only took one horse to pull the cab. Captain went out with Jerry all that first morning. In the afternoon, I was put into the cab.

Jerry made sure the collar and bridle fitted well. There was no bearing rein this time. What a blessing that was!

Jerry drove me to the main street, where lots of other horse cabs were queuing up and waiting for customers. We pulled up at the back of the line.

As I was a new horse, lots of the other drivers came to see me.

"Too smart for this job," said one.

"Be better pulling a funeral coach," laughed a second man.

"He won't last," remarked another.

Jerry just smiled. "Jack will make a good cab horse," he said. "He's an aristocrat. I can tell."

The first week of my life as a cab horse was difficult. I was not used to London; the noise, the hurry, the crowds of horses, carts and carriages.

A London Cab Horse

I was not used to London.

But I learned to trust Jerry. He was as good a driver as I had ever known. And he cared for his horses as well as his family.

He soon found out that I was willing to work hard and always do my best. He never used his whip on me in anger.

It didn't take very long before my new master and I understood each other as well as a horse and man can do.

In the stable, Captain and I were well cared for. We had good food and plenty of fresh water.

But one of the nicest things was that we had a day off to rest on Sundays. We loved our day of rest and it was on those days that I learned about Captain's past.

Captain had been a warhorse. His owner had been an officer in the cavalry.

Captain explained how he had been taught to charge forward at full speed when a bugle sounded. I asked him whether he had been frightened about going into battle.

"Not very much," he replied. "We always loved to hear the bugle call and to be called out for duty. We were keen to start, though sometimes we had to stand for hours before a battle. But when the order came, we charged forward as eagerly as if there were no cannon balls whirling through the air about our ears."

Captain said he had gone into action with his master many times and had never been wounded.

"I saw many horses injured," he continued. "We had to leave them behind on the battlefield. But I never feared for my own life. My master was so brave and cheerful; I never thought of being hurt. I trusted him completely. I would have charged into a thousand men if he had asked me to.

"I saw many brave men fall from their saddles. I heard their pitiful cries and groans. And I often had to turn suddenly, to avoid treading on an injured man who had fallen to the ground.

"But no, I never truly felt fear or terror until one special day. I shall never forget it."

At that point Captain paused for a while and took a deep breath before continuing. I could see he was thinking about something quite dreadful.

Chapter 22
The Charge of the Light Brigade

"On this particular day, we fought a most dreadful battle," said Captain. "I didn't know what it was called then, but I heard later that its name was the Battle of Balaclava, in a place called The Crimea. The story I am about to tell you concerns one charge in that battle.

"They called it 'The Charge of the Light Brigade'. The Light Brigade was the name of my owner's cavalry unit.

"It was an autumn morning and, as usual, an hour before daybreak, all the horses were readied for the day's work. All the men stood by their horses and waited for their orders.

There were six hundred riders and six hundred horses. I had never seen so many men and horses gathered together in one place.

"As the light got brighter, there seemed to be great excitement among the officers. And before long, we heard the firing of the enemy's cannons.

"Then one of the officers rode up and gave the order for the men to mount their horses. In a second, they were all in the saddle.

"We horses stood absolutely still, except for an occasional toss of the head. We waited for the touch of our masters' heels, to tell us to move.

"My dear master and I were at the front of the line. He stroked the back of my head more than he had ever done before. It was as if his mind had wandered and he was thinking of something else. I knew that he was very nervous.

"I can't tell you all that happened on that day. I remember that the battle went on for hours. We made many charges at the enemy.

"And I remember every detail of the last charge of all. We had to charge down a valley, right in front of the enemy's cannons.

"We were all used to the roar of the guns, the rattle of musket fire and the shot flying about our ears. But never had I seen such fire as that day! There were cannon to the left, cannon to the right and cannon in front of us.

"Many a brave man went down and many a horse fell, flinging his rider to the ground. Hundreds of riderless horses scattered across the battlefield. Some horses refused to leave the field, even after their masters had been killed. Some rejoined the charge, just to be with the other horses.

"My dear master was standing up in his stirrups with his sword raised high as he urged everyone on.

"Then I heard a musket ball whiz just over my head. I felt my master suddenly fall back into the saddle. He had been hit. But I never heard him utter a cry.

"The sword dropped from my master's hand. Then he slipped from the saddle and fell to the ground. Other horses and riders charged passed us, and I was quickly driven from the place where my master had fallen.

"I didn't want to leave him to be trampled by all the charging horses behind. But there was nothing I could do.

"Then another cavalry officer whose horse had been injured leapt onto my back. I rejoined the battle but it was all too late. The charge was a complete disaster. The enemy won the day.

"The horses that still had riders now returned in the direction they had come. Some of the horses were so badly wounded they could scarcely move.

"Some noble creatures tried to drag

We waited for the touch of our masters' heels.

themselves back to camp on three legs. The battlefield echoed to the sound of men and horses crying from their wounds.

"After the battle, the wounded men were collected and brought back to camp. The poor wounded horses were put out of their misery. A few with minor injuries were brought back, and looked after.

"Most of the six hundred horses that went out that morning never returned. And I never saw my beloved master again.

"I carried new masters into battle on several occasions after that, but I never loved them as much as my old master. I was wounded once, but not seriously. And when the war was over I returned to England."

And there the old horse finished his story.

I told Captain that I had heard people say war and battle were great things.

"Ah," said Captain, "people who say that were never in a battle. War is a terrible thing. Thousands of good, brave men and horses were killed or crippled for life in the battles I saw."

I asked Captain if he knew what they had been fighting about.

"No," he said, "that is more than a horse can understand."

My master urged everyone on.

Chapter 23
A Trip to the Country

I never knew a better man than my new master. Jerry was as gentle, strong and kind as John Manly. And he was so good tempered that very few people could pick a quarrel with him.

Jerry's family helped him take very good care of us – and his cab. His son, Harry, helped with the stable work. And he was as good at the work as a much older boy.

Polly and Dolly came to the yard each morning, to help with the cab. They brushed and beat the cushions, polished the coachwork and rubbed the windows until they sparkled.

They were always laughing together. And their happiness never failed to put Captain and I in a good mood.

Jerry was not one to hurry through life at the expense of his horses.

One day when we were at work, two wild-looking young men came out of an inn close to where the cabs and their drivers waited for customers.

"Here, cabby!" one shouted. "Look sharp. We're late. If you can get to Victoria Station in time to catch the one o'clock train, I'll give you an extra shilling."

"I'll take you, gentlemen," replied Jerry, "but I shall go at the normal speed. My horse is not a steam engine."

Another cabby called Larry heard the conversation. He hurried forward to speak to the two young men. "I'm your man," he said, "I'll crack the whip and get you there in time."

The men got aboard and Larry gave his horse a sharp crack with the whip. The poor horse clattered away at speed.

I knew that horse would not be working for much longer. It would soon be crippled by being forced to gallop through the rough, cobbled streets of London.

Sometimes there were important occasions when Jerry did ask me for more speed. Once we came upon a young man who had been injured in an accident in the street. We found him lying unconscious.

Jerry ran over and picked him up, and put him in the cab. Then we raced off to the local hospital at top speed. It saved his life.

It was always difficult to drive quickly in London during the day. The streets were so full of traffic; rich people's four-wheeled carriages, omnibuses, carts, vans, trucks and great farm wagons, bringing food to the city.

But a good driver and horse could make light work of it. I had a good mouth. That meant I could be guided by the gentlest pull on the bit. So Jerry and I nipped in and out of the busy traffic quicker than most cabs.

Jerry, of course, never worked on a Sunday. He liked to give his horses a rest and be with his family. But one Sunday in early summer, Polly ran into the stable looking quite upset.

Polly told Jerry that her friend Dinah Brown had just received a letter, telling her that her mother was seriously ill.

I heard Polly say that Dinah's mother lived ten miles away in the country and had no money to pay for a cab.

Jerry didn't hesitate. He hitched me to the cab and soon we were out in the country, taking Dinah to her mother.

The smell of the sweet air, fresh grass and wildflowers reminded me of the old days. It was wonderful!

A Trip to the Country

"Here, cabby!"

Dinah's family lived in a small farmhouse by a beautiful meadow. When we got there, Dinah went in to see her mother while Jerry removed my harness and bridle. "I've got a rare treat for you, my boy," he said.

He led me into the meadow and let me go. I was so excited to be back in a grassy meadow. I didn't know whether to eat, or roll in the lush grass, or just lie down and fall asleep in the sunshine. In the end, I did all of them in turn.

He led me into the meadow.

A Trip to the Country

I had not been in a meadow since I left poor Ginger.

Jerry sat on a grassy bank beneath a shady tree. He watched me enjoy myself as he ate the bread and cheese Polly had packed for him.

Later, he picked some wildflowers and tied them together with a piece of ivy. Then it was time to take Dinah back to London again. She was very grateful that we had brought her to see her mother.

What a wonderful Sunday we had! When we got home, Jerry gave the wildflowers to Polly. She was thrilled.

Chapter 24
Winter in London

Summer turned to autumn and then winter arrived with a chilly bite! There was snow, sleet or rain almost every day for weeks.

We horses felt it very much. When it is dry and cold, a couple of good thick rugs will keep us warm. But when we're soaked by rain or snow, we are quickly chilled to the bone.

Some of the cab drivers had waterproof clothes. But most were so poor that they could not protect themselves, or their horses. Many a horse and man suffered that winter.

The streets became very slippery with frost and ice in the cold weather. This was very dangerous for us horses. We struggled to keep to our feet and worried about falling down. It made our work much harder.

Jerry only worked us for a few hours each day when the weather was bad. And we always went back to stables that were warm and dry. But the other horses were often out all day and night.

Polly always made sure Jerry had plenty to eat. Sometimes we'd see her peep around the corner, to see if her husband was on the taxi rank. If he was, she would hurry home and bring back some hot soup or a steaming pudding.

One cold, windy day, a gentleman wanting a cab came up to Jerry when he was in the middle of drinking a bowl of soup.

Jerry was about to put the soup aside when the man held up his hand. "No, finish your soup first," he said. "I can wait."

When the soup was finished, Jerry drove the man to his home in the south of the city. Several times after that, the same gentleman took our cab.

He was very fond of horses and dogs, and whenever we took him to his front door, two or three dogs would rush out to meet him.

Sometimes he came around to the front of the cab, to pat me. I heard him say once, "This horse has a good master and he deserves it."

On another day, we were taking the gentleman into the city. He spotted another cab driver cruelly whipping his horse.

"If you don't stop that," he shouted, "I'll have you taken to court for behaving so brutally to your animal!"

"No, finish your soup first."

"Mind your own business!" the cab driver snarled. But he stopped whipping his horse, for he did not want to be charged with cruelty.

As we drove away, the gentleman spoke to Jerry. "The trouble with this world," he said, "is that people only think about their own business. They don't bother to stand up to someone who is doing something wrong, like that rude man."

"I wish there were more gentlemen like you, sir," answered Jerry.

"I believe," said the man, "that if we see something cruel being done, we must try and stop it. If we don't, we are as guilty as the person who is doing the cruel act."

Chapter 25
A Great Shock

On another freezing day, an old cab drove up alongside the place where Jerry and I waited for work.

The horse was a worn-out chestnut color. Her coat was rough and hadn't been groomed for many a day. Her bones stuck out horribly. The horse was very unsteady on her bent, skinny legs.

As the cab stopped, the horse turned to look at me. There was a sad and hopeless expression in her gentle eyes.

Suddenly, I realized that I had seen the horse before.

She stared at me for a moment and said, "Black Beauty, is that you?"

It was Ginger! But how she had changed. Her beautifully arched and glossy neck was now straight and dull. And all the joints in her legs were swollen.

Her face, once so full of spirit and life, was

It was Ginger!

now full of suffering and pain. She could hardly breathe without coughing.

Our drivers were now standing together a little way off, so I moved closer to Ginger. She had a sad tale to tell.

I learned she had stayed resting in Lord White's field and gradually recovered from her leg weakness. She had been sold to another gentleman as soon as she was fit, but the old injury returned when she was asked to work hard.

"After that," said Ginger, "I was sold time and time again, each time getting a worse job. Finally, I was bought by a man called Nicholas Skinner, who runs several cabs. He is more interested in money that looking after his horses. He knows of my weakness but is determined to get his money's worth out of me. So I just get whipped and beaten, without a thought for my injured leg. I'm worked seven days a week. I never have a single day's rest."

I reminded Ginger of the days when she used to stand up for herself if she was mistreated.

"I did once," replied Ginger. "But it is no use. Men are stronger, and if they are cruel and have no feelings for us horses, there's nothing we can do about it. We've just got to bear it until the end. I wish the end would come. I wish I was dead."

Ginger's words troubled me greatly. I put my nose to hers.

"You and Merrylegs were the only friends I ever had," she said.

"I know. I know," I replied. "I wished we'd never been split up."

At that moment, Ginger's driver leapt back on the cab. With a violent tug on the reins, he drove her away. I felt so terribly sad.

A few days later I passed a cart carrying a dead horse. Its head hung out of the back of the cart. The sight was too dreadful.

It was a chestnut horse with a long thin neck. I was sure it was Ginger. I hoped it was, for then her troubles would be over.

I saw a great deal of cruelty to horses in London. I felt very sad when I saw small ponies straining with heavy loads, or staggering under heavy blows from some cruel boy.

Of course, all horses weren't treated badly. Many young working lads grew very fond of their animals.

There was a grocery boy who had an old and very ugly pony. But oh, how he loved that

The boy and his pony were inseparable friends.

animal! He and his pony were inseparable friends. The pony followed his master like a pet dog. And when he got into his grocery cart, the pony would trot off without a whip or a word.

There was also an old man who used to come up our street delivering coal. He and his horse used to plod up and down the streets together.

The horse didn't need to be told to stop at a particular house. He knew all the houses where he had to deliver coal. He and his master were like old partners who understood each other perfectly.

Jerry used to say what a comfort it was to think how happy a horse could be, even in a thankless job such as delivering groceries, or coal.

Chapter 26
More Tragedy

Captain and I become great friends. He was a noble old fellow and very good company.

One day, he and Jerry took some customers to the railway station. They were on their way back when Jerry saw a huge wagon coming towards him, loaded with barrels of beer. It was pulled by two powerful horses.

The driver was drunk and lashing the horses with his whip. As they broke into a trot, the man seemed to lose control of them.

The street was full of traffic and the horses were going faster and faster. The next moment, the wagon collided with Jerry's cab.

Both the cab's wheels on one side were torn off and the cab itself was tipped over. The wooden shafts splintered and poor Captain was dragged to the ground. One of the shafts ran into his side.

Jerry was thrown onto the road. He was badly bruised, but everyone said afterwards

More Tragedy

The wagon collided with Jerry's cab.

that he was lucky not to be killed.

When Captain got up, it was seen that he was badly cut and knocked about. There was a lot of blood on his side.

Jerry and the vet did their best for Captain. But the poor horse would never pull a cab again.

Jerry blamed the drunken man for the accident. "If only drunken people would break their own bones," he said, angrily. "But they never injure themselves. It's always the innocent who suffer!"

Captain did partly recover from his injuries. But he was a very old horse and was always in pain. There was talk of him being sold off as a carthorse, doomed to hard labor until he finally dropped dead.

Jerry refused to allow it.

"How can I send an old friend to such an end?" he cried. "Captain has been a wonderful and faithful servant. I will never let it happen."

A few days later, I went out on a job. When I returned Captain was gone.

I knew what had happened. The kindly Jerry had put Captain out of his misery.

He would suffer no more.

Chapter 27
New Year's Eve

The New Year is a happy time for most people. But it is no holiday for cab drivers and their horses. There are so many parties to collect people from, late at night. It is very hard work.

Sometimes cab drivers and their horses have to wait for hours in the rain or frost, shivering with cold while everyone else is merrily dancing the night away.

I wonder if the beautiful ladies at these parties ever think of the weary drivers waiting outside, and the horses standing still until their legs get stiff with cold.

One New Year Jerry caught a dreadful cough and cold. But he still went out to work.

Jerry and I took two gentlemen to a party in the center of London. We dropped them off at nine o'clock and they told Jerry to pick them up at eleven.

As the clock struck eleven we were back at

the door to collect them. A servant came and told Jerry that they would be delayed. So we waited.

Midnight passed and still the two men had not come out.

The icy wind cut into my sides. Snow swirled around us. There was nowhere to shelter and we were very cold.

Jerry got off the cab and covered me with a blanket. Then he walked about a bit, stamping his feet and wrapping his arms about his body to try and keep warm.

The clock struck one. Jerry knocked on the door again and asked if the men were coming.

"Oh, yes," said the servant. "But you'll have to wait just a little longer."

Jerry sat down in the cab again. His cough was getting worse and worse.

Finally, at two o'clock, the men came out. Jerry drove them home. It was a journey of more than two miles. My legs were numb with cold and I stumbled several times.

When the men got out, they never said they were sorry to have kept us waiting. But they did complain about the amount Jerry charged for the journey. Yet, he hadn't charged a penny more or less than his normal fare.

Snow swirled around us.

By the time we got home, Jerry could hardly speak. His cough was dreadful. But he still had time to rub me down, put out some fresh straw and give me some oats before thinking of himself.

*

It was late the next morning before anyone came to the stable. It was Harry who came to feed me. He wasn't whistling happily, as he usually did. And there was no sign of Jerry.

At noon Dolly came with my midday feed. She was crying. I soon found out that Jerry was dangerously ill.

The next day, another cab driver came into the stable while Harry was cleaning up.

"How is your father?" he asked.

"Very bad," said Harry. "He couldn't be much worse. The doctor says the fever will turn one way or the other by tonight."

The cab driver returned the following morning.

"How is he?" he asked, again.

"He's better," said Harry. "The doctor thinks he'll make it."

"Thank God," he said. "If any man is strong

"How is your father?"

enough to beat the fever, it's him. Keep him warm."

Jerry grew slowly better, but the doctor warned him never to go back to driving cabs again if he wanted to live to be an old man.

A few days later, I heard Dolly give Harry some important news. She was very excited.

"We're leaving London!" she said. "We're going to live in the country! Mrs. Fowler, a friend of Mother's, has said that now Father has to give up his job, we can all go and live in a small cottage near her."

"Will Father be able to work there?" asked Harry.

"Yes!" said Dolly. "He is to be Mrs. Fowler's groom and coachman. And she's said that whenever it is cold or wet, there's a young boy who will drive the coach for him."

But there was bad news for me. Mrs. Fowler had no room for any more horses. I would have to be sold.

This time I was to go and work for a miller who ground corn for local bakers.

The day when I had to leave came quickly. Jerry, Polly, Dolly and Harry all came to see me.

"Poor old boy," said Dolly, stroking my neck

affectionately. "I wish we could take you with us."

She kissed me on the nose and began to cry. Then she ran off, as she couldn't bear to say goodbye.

Harry and Jerry stroked me too, but said nothing. They seemed very sad. A short time later, I was led away to my new place.

145

Chapter 28
A Miller's Horse

The miller I went to work for was a friend of Jerry's. He treated me well. He accepted that I was an old horse and couldn't haul heavy loads.

But Jake, the miller's driver, treated me differently. He always loaded my cart with as much grain as possible.

"Best make one journey rather than two," he used to say.

He also used a bearing rein to keep my head up. It was agonizing.

One day my cart was fully loaded and I was struggling to get up a steep hill. It was too much for me. I had to stop several times to catch my breath.

Each time I stopped, Jake whipped me on. "Get on, you lazy fellow," he shouted, "or I'll make you move!"

The pain of that thick whip was terrible. It wasn't fair! I was doing my best and still being punished. It took the heart out of me.

My cart was fully loaded.

A lady saw Jake whipping me. "Don't punish that horse any more!" she said firmly. "He's doing his best."

"If he can't get up this hill by doing his best," cried Jake, "then he must do better, ma'am."

The lady wasn't going to give up. She saw that Jake wasn't a really cruel man. He just didn't realize what he was doing.

"Let me show you how to get the horse to go up that hill," she said.

"Anything for a lady," answered Jake.

The lady walked up close to me and undid the bearing rein. Suddenly, I could breathe properly again. What a comfort it was to be able to drop my head for a while!

I tossed my head several times to get rid of the stiffness.

"Poor fellow," said the lady, stroking my nose, "that's what you wanted, wasn't it?"

Then she spoke to Jake. "Now, let the horse have his head and speak to him gently. I'm sure he'll get you up this hill."

Jake took the rein again. "Come on, now" he said, quietly.

I put my head down and threw my whole weight into pulling the cart.

The load began to move. Slowly, I went up

"Let the horse have his head."

the hill. I stopped for a breath a little further up. This time he didn't whip me. The lady had been walking up the hill beside us. She came over and patted my neck.

"You see," she said, "the horse was quite willing when you gave him the chance. I imagine he was a fine horse once. He has seen better days, that is for sure."

Jake was grateful for the lady's advice. But when she told him never to use the bearing rein again, he wasn't so sure. "The other drivers will laugh at me," he said. "It's the fashion to use the bearing rein."

With that, the lady shook her head and walked away.

"That was a real lady," Jake said to himself after she had gone. "She spoke to me as if I was a gentleman. The least I can do is to try what she said."

He did use the bearing rein at times after that, but he always took it off when we came to a hill.

It was about this time that I started to suffer with eye problems.

The stable I now lived in was quite dark, with only one small window. It weakened my sight.

A Miller's Horse

Whenever I came out into the glare of the daylight, it was very painful to my eyes. Several times I stumbled and could hardly see where I was going.

Some horses go blind from this problem. If I had stayed in that stable, I think I would have gone blind.

But the miller saw how old and weak I had become. He bought a younger horse and sold me back into the cab trade.

I shall never forget my new master. He had dark, beady eyes and a hooked nose. His mouth was so full of teeth that he looked like a bulldog. His voice was so rough that it sounded like cart wheels grinding over cobblestones. He was Nicholas Skinner.

Skinner was the man who had made Ginger's life a nightmare. Now he was going to teach me just how utterly miserable a cab horse's life could be.

Chapter 29
Skinner

Skinner had a rough and ready team of cab drivers. He was hard on his men and, in turn, they were hard on the horses. Skinner and his men drove me until I almost dropped.

Skinner thought nothing of a making a horse drive fifteen miles into the country and back in one morning.

He never asked the passengers to get out of the cab on a steep hill. Neither did he slow down on a hot summer day.

Jerry always gave his horses plenty of time off to rest. Skinner and his men worked us seven days a week.

Skinner himself had a cruel whip that often drew blood. He would whip me under my belly and flip the lash over my head sometimes, if he thought I was not moving fast enough.

My life was now nothing but pain and misery. I wished, like Ginger had, to drop dead and escape my dreadful life.

My life was now nothing but pain and misery.

One day my wish was very nearly granted.

Skinner and I had been waiting at the railway station when a man booked our cab for a journey to his house. There was a lady, a little boy and girl, and a lot of luggage with him.

"Papa," said the girl, "I'm not sure this poor old horse can take us all and the luggage too. He looks so weak and worn out."

"Oh, he's alright," said Skinner. "He's strong enough."

A station porter agreed with the girl that perhaps they should take a second cab for the luggage.

"No," said Skinner, "the horse can do it. Put the luggage on the roof."

"Oh, Papa!" said the little girl. "Do take a second cab. I am sure it's too much for the horse. It's cruel."

"Nonsense," said the girl's father. "Stop making a fuss. The driver knows his business and he says the horse can take it."

So the rest of the luggage was piled up on the roof and the family got into the cab.

Skinner cracked the whip and drove us all out of the station.

The load was very heavy and I hadn't eaten anything for hours. I did my best but it wasn't enough. I was soon exhausted. It was too much for me.

Suddenly, I felt dizzy. My feet slipped from under me and I fell heavily to the ground. I couldn't move. I just lay perfectly still where I had fallen. I thought I was going to die.

I heard confusion around me. People were shouting at each other and the luggage was being unloaded.

I heard the little girl say, "Oh, that poor horse, it's all our fault!"

I thought I was going to die.

A man knelt down and undid my bridle and harness. Someone else said, "The horse is dead. He'll never work again."

I don't know how long I lay there, but a kindly person stroked my nose and encouraged me to get up. I eventually staggered to my feet and was led back to my stable.

A vet was called and he told Skinner what he thought. "The accident was caused by too much work. This horse needs six months off before he can pull a cab again. There's not an ounce of strength in him."

"I haven't got the time to see if he'll get better," snarled Skinner. "He either works or I send him to market . . . not than anyone would buy a horse in his condition."

And so, a few days later, I was sent off to market again. I had no hopes of ever finding a kind owner. But anything would be better than working for Skinner.

Chapter 30
A Kind Farmer

At the market, I found myself with the oldest and most broken-down horses I had ever seen. Most were lame. Some looked like walking skeletons.

A thoughtful owner might have taken one look and decided it would be kinder to put us all out of our misery.

The market was divided into different areas. The cheapest and sickest-looking horses occupied one part. That's where I was. The better horses were in another area.

I was very surprised when a wealthy farmer with a young boy at his side appeared in our part of the market.

"There's a horse that's seen better days," said the farmer, pointing at me.

"Poor old fellow," said the boy, sadly. "Grandpa, do you think he pulled carriages when he was young?"

"Oh, for sure," answered the farmer. "He

might have been anything when he was young. Just look at the noble shape of his head and shoulders."

The boy put his hand out and stroked the back of my neck. "He really is a poor old fellow, isn't he grandpa," said the boy. "Couldn't we buy him and make him young again, like we did with that chestnut mare?"

"My dear boy," said the farmer, "I can't make all old horses young again. That mare was half-dead when we saw her at market. But she still had the will to live. I think this horse is too far gone.'

"No, he's not!" protested the boy. "He's not that old. We could make him better."

The man selling the horses in our part of the market heard what the boy said, and turned to the farmer. "The boy's right, you know," he said. "That horse is not as old as he looks. He's been a cab horse for some time and just got overworked. Six months in a grassy meadow and he'd be as right as rain again. You won't find a friendlier horse."

The farmer laughed and hugged his grandson. "You're a kindly, thoughtful boy. Yes, we'll take him in and see how he turns out."

That evening I was taken to the man's home

"That horse has seen better days."

and put in a meadow thick with lush, green grass. I could hardly believe my luck

My new master's name was Mr. Goodwin. He put his grandson, who was called Willie, in charge of me.

The boy was very proud to have his own horse to look after. He visited me every day and made sure I always had food and water. He didn't try to ride me at first because I was still too weak.

That winter I got stronger every day. By the time the spring flowers were growing in the meadow, I felt better than I had in years.

Mr. Goodwin said it was time to see if I was fit enough to pull a small carriage. I was happy to be back in harness and I pulled Mr. Goodwin and his grandson around his farm. My legs were a little stiff but I did the job well.

"See!" said the boy. "He's growing younger and stronger by the day. By midsummer he'll be as good as the old chestnut mare. I'm so glad you bought him."

"So am I, my boy," said the farmer. "But the horse has you to thank for his recovery."

The man then spoke seriously to his grandson. "You'll be off back to school soon and you won't have time to look after the horse. We

A Kind Farmer

I felt better than I had in years.

must find him a good place to live before the summer is out, just like we did with the chestnut horse."

I was sad to discover that I was to be sent to yet another home. Yet, I had found out that Mr. Goodwin often went to the market to rescue sick horses. He helped them recover and then found good homes for them.

Chapter 31
A Wonderful Surprise

It came as something of a surprise to find out that my new home was just a few miles away. On the way there, I thought how familiar the countryside looked.

When we reached the house, I was led around to the stable at the back. Mr. Goodwin and Willie said goodbye and left. I was sorry to see them go. Willie promised to come and see me when he had his next holiday.

Then I was all alone. I wondered who my new owner was.

A few minutes later, the stable door opened and a man came in.

"Well, you're a lovely horse, aren't you," he said. 'Let's have a look at you."

"Well, what about that!" he said, with a look of surprise on his face. "You've got a white star on your nose, old boy. What a coincidence, I once knew a lovely horse that had a white star like yours. I often wonder where he is now."

A puzzled look crossed his face. He stepped back to get a better look at me.

"A white sock too," he said, staring at my one white foot. "The other horse had a white sock. How strange. He also had a tiny patch of white hair on his back. I wonder . . ."

As he said that, he walked closer to me and looked down my back. "My goodness!" he exclaimed. "A white patch!"

The man came round to my front again. "Black Beauty? Is it you, Beauty? It is, isn't it!"

The man stepped back. "Beauty, don't you remember me? Little Joe Green. Squire Gordon's stable boy. Remember how I nearly killed you? I forgot to cover you with a blanket after your ride to fetch the doctor for Squire Gordon's wife."

The man seemed overjoyed to see me.

I could not say that I recognized him, for he was no longer the boy I had once known. Now he was a grown man, with black whiskers and a very deep voice. I did know him though, and I was so pleased that he knew me.

I put my nose close to his face and nuzzled him affectionately. I never saw a man so happy to see a horse.

A Wonderful Surprise

"Well, you're a lovely horse, aren't you."

"Well, I never!" said Joe. "I never thought I'd see you again."

He suddenly stood up and ran out of the stable. He returned a few minutes later with two women scurrying behind him.

They were also much older than when I had seen them last. But I recognized them both.

They were Flora and Jessie, the two daughters of Squire Gordon, who had played with Merrylegs, Ginger and I when we were all young.

"Black Beauty!" cried Flora. "It really is you!

The two women threw their arms around my neck and gave me a huge hug.

I realized at last where I was. This had been the home of Mr. Blomefield, who was once the minister of the village church.

This was where Merrylegs and Joe Green had gone to live, when Squire Gordon went abroad with his wife and I went to Lord White's.

I was back in the village where I had spent my youth. Everyone was delighted and excited to see me. It seemed that Mr. Blomefield had died, but his two sons had married the Squire's two daughters. And now they all lived at Mr. Blomefield's old property.

They had children of their own now.

A Wonderful Surprise

Suddenly, three youngsters rushed into the stable to see the new arrival. They jumped and climbed all over me.

"Be careful, children," said Flora. "Beauty's an old horse now. You must treat him with care."

I didn't mind. I was overjoyed to play with the children. It made me feel young again."

Then Joe spoke again, in a mysterious way. "We've forgotten the others. Do you think Beauty will remember them?"

"Let's take him out and see," said Flora, excitedly.

They led me out of the stable and into a meadow where some other horses were grazing.

"I bet Beauty does remember them," said Jessie.

"But it's been years," replied Flora.

They led me to the corner of the meadow and there, cooling themselves off in a pond beneath some chestnut trees, stood two horses. Of course, I remembered them. How could I forget them?

It was Merrylegs and Ginger!

It was Merrylegs and Ginger!

Chapter 32
Together Again

I could hardly believe my eyes.

I had often wondered if Merrylegs, who was a little older than me but younger than Ginger, was still alive. And here he was, as friendly and happy as ever.

As for Ginger, I was so sure that she had died. When I saw the body of the chestnut horse being carried through the streets of London, I was convinced it was Ginger. How glad I was that I had been mistaken!

I trotted into the pond and joined them. We touched noses and neighed with pleasure to be back together again after so many years.

Ginger looked so different from when I had seen her pulling that cab in London. She had put on some weight and her ribs no longer stuck out.

But how had she found her way here?

Ginger soon told me that Skinner had sent her to be sold at the market. And there Mr.

Goodwin had rescued her, just as he had saved me.

In my worst moments of pulling cabs with Skinner in the chill of the London winter, I had dreamed of standing in the cool waters of a pond in a summer meadow with my friends, Merrylegs and Ginger.

I never really imagined it would ever happen again. But now, as the sun made the pond sparkle on that warm summer evening, it was as if we had never been separated.

We were no longer young and able to gallop around the field, and roll over in the grass like youngsters.

But we were happy again. And we would grow old together. This would be a last happy home for all of us. We had a safe, good home, for the rest of our lives.

Together Again

We were happy again.

The End

Helyntion
Hogan Wyllt

Mari Jones-Williams

Argraffiad cyntaf: 2012

ⓗ Mari Jones-Williams/Gwasg Carreg Gwalch

Rhif rhyngwladol: 978-1-84527-372-9

Mae'r cyhoeddwyr yn cydnabod cefnogaeth ariannol
Cyngor Llyfrau Cymru

Cynllun clawr: Sion Ilar

Cyhoeddwyd gan Wasg Carreg Gwalch,
12 Iard yr Orsaf, Llanrwst, Conwy, LL26 0EH.
Ffôn: 01492 642031 Ffacs: 01492 641502
e-bost: llyfrau@carreg-gwalch.com
lle ar y we: www.carreg-gwalch.com

Diolch i Dylan Iorwerth a Golwg am roi lle i'r Hogan adrodd ei hanesion lliwgar nôl yn 1997, i Dyfan a chriw Golwg bymtheng mlynedd wedyn am ddod o hyd iddyn nhw ar gyfer y llyfr yma ac i Wasg Carreg Gwalch am gytuno i'w hatgyfodi; diolch i bawb fu'n gwarchod y plantos wrth i mi drio cyrraedd dedlein (arall) a Nia fy ngolygydd siriol am ei hamynedd di-ball a'i nerfau dur! Diolch Bren am fy mwydo, fy nyfrio a jest am beidio gofyn . . .

Genod: rhowch eich ymennydd mewn gêr isel a mwynhewch. Llin a Leis: gobeithio bydd rhai i ddilyn i chi, ond am fy annog i'w 'sgwennu, ei darllen a'i licio, mae hon i Shon.